KT-436-570

WALKER BOOKS
AND SUBSIDIARIES
LONDON • BOSTON • SYDNEY

First published 2002 by Walker Books Ltd
87 Vauxhall Walk, London SE11 5HJ

10 9 8 7 6 5 4 3 2 1

© 2002 Ed Boxall

This book has been typeset in Gill Sans MT Schlbk

Printed in Hong Kong

All rights reserved

British Library Cataloguing in Publication Data:
a catalogue record for this book is available
from the British Library

ISBN 0-7445-8894-4

Francis
the Scaredy Cat

Ed Boxall

FALKIRK COUNCIL
LIBRARY SUPPORT
FOR SCHOOLS

This is
Francis.

Francis likes to read stories.

He loves bubble baths,

and
hunting
carrots.

Best of all,
Francis loves Ben,
with his kind hands
and voice as familiar
as pillows and
pyjamas.

Francis is a happy cat,
but he has a secret.
A secret even from Ben.
Francis is a scaredy-cat.

Francis is afraid of the dark.
And most of all, he is afraid
of the whispery hissy monster
he hears in the big tree in
the garden on stormy nights.

One evening, Ben was late home
and Francis was all alone.
The wind got louder
and the storm got wilder.
The night grew darker and darker.
It became so dark that Francis
wasn't sure if his eyes were
open or closed.

The tree whooshed and crashed outside. Francis heard the whispery monster hissing.

Suddenly Francis had a terrible thought: what if the monster had captured Ben?

Francis
knew what
he had to do.
He peeped
outside at
the dark night.
He crept into
the garden.

He climbed
the big tree
to rescue his friend.

He was shaking,
from the tip
of his wet
nose to
the end of
his fluffy
tail.

**But he looked down
and his scaredy head spun
and his scaredy legs went
wobbly under him.**

And poor Francis
was stuck, with
something hissing
behind him.

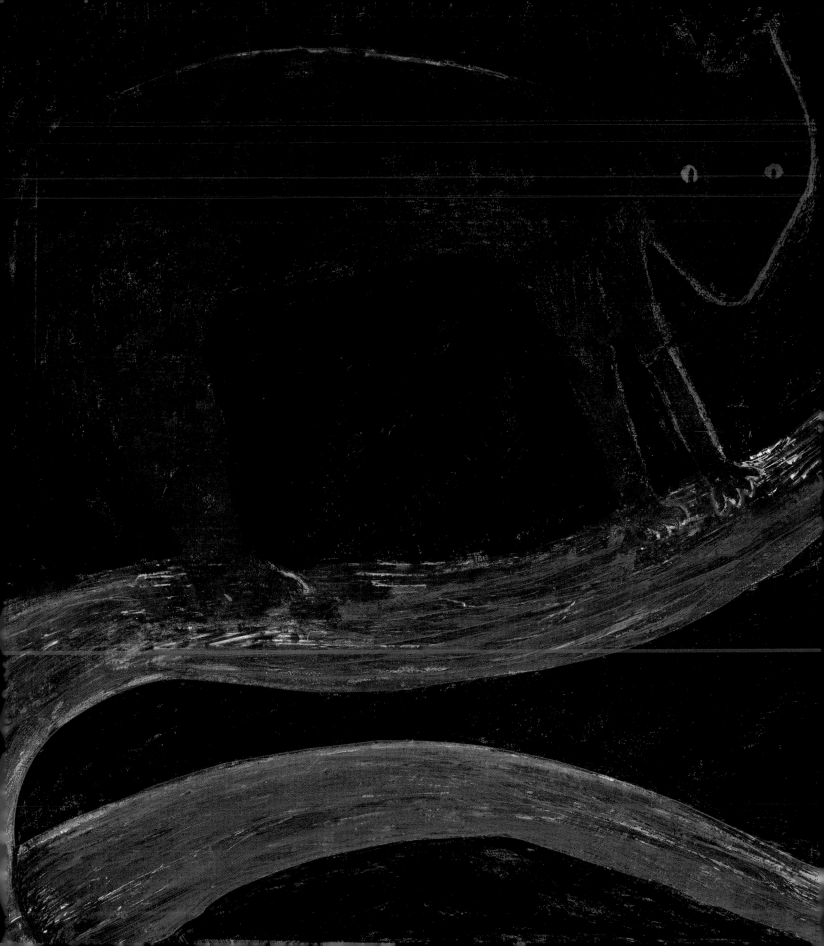

Francis turned and
saw two bright eyes
glaring at him ...

but he stood up,
ready to fight.

The hissy monster
leapt out of the shadows,
and Francis saw ...

a cat,
a big cat,
a wild cat,
but a cat
like him.

A cat with a kind face,
who led Francis gently
down the tree, showing
him where to put each
step, down to the ground
where he found ...

Ben, with his big kind hands
and his voice as familiar
as pillows and pyjamas.

Ben hugged Francis.

Francis hugged Ben.

FALKIRK COUNCIL
LIBRARY SUPPORT
FOR SCHOOLS

D

058423

THE HENLEY COLLEGE LIBRARY

WITHDRAWN